RUFUS AT WORK

TORY AND NORMAN TABER

Walker & Company
New York

I am Rufus.

This is my girl, Posy.

Sometimes Posy says, "Rufus, fat cat, what good are you?"

Could it be that she doesn't know how much I do?

I work so hard,
it makes me dizzy!

Without me, how would Posy know when it's time to wake up?

Who would help her
with breakfast?

I keep the sun off the rug.

I straighten my stripes.

I wake up Finn.
He expects it.

While Posy is away at school, I guard the birdbath,

and decorate the neighbor's car.

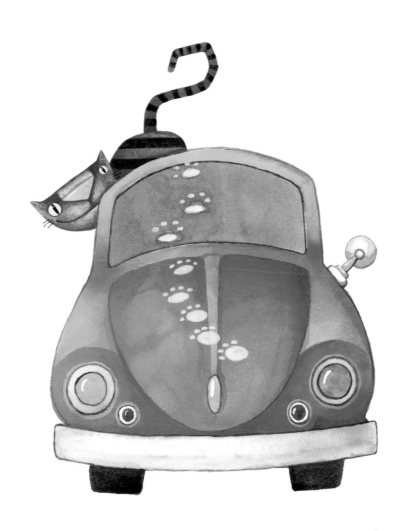

Without me,

who would exercise the chickens?

Then there's the gardening:
I prune the catnip,

and listen for moles . . . for a
very long time.

When Posy comes home from school, I need to welcome her. She requires a great deal of entertaining. It's all very hard work!

At the end of such a long day,
sometimes I don't have much
energy left. It's difficult to help
Posy with her homework, but
I do. It's all part of the job.

So when she says, "Rufus, fat cat,
what good are you?" I purr,
"You're only human, Posy my girl,
you wouldn't understand."

To our girls, Zoe and Liz

First published in the United States of America in 2005 by
Walker Publishing Company, Inc.
Distributed to the trade by Holtzbrinck Publishers

For information about permission to reproduce selections from
this book, write to Permissions, Walker & Company,
104 Fifth Avenue, New York, New York 10011.

Library of Congress Cataloging-in-Publication Data
available upon request
ISBN 0-8027-8984-6 (hardcover)
ISBN-13 978-0-8027-8984-6 (hardcover)
ISBN 0-8027-8985-4 (reinforced)
ISBN-13 978-0-8027-8985-3 (reinforced)

The artist used acrylic paints on Arches hot-press watercolor paper
to create the illustrations for this book.

 Produced by Design Press, a division of the

Savannah College of Art and Design

www.designpressbooks.com

Book design by Anna Marlis Burgard and Angela Rojas

Visit Walker & Company's Web site at www.walkeryoungreaders.com

Printed in Hong Kong

2 4 6 8 10 9 7 5 3 1